RUMPELSTILTSKIN

AND OTHER ANGRY IMPS WITH RATHER UNUSUAL NAMES

Amelia Carruthers

ORIGINS OF FAIRY TALES
FROM AROUND THE WORLD

Copyright © 2015 Pook Press
An imprint of Read Publishing Ltd.
Home Farm, 44 Evesham Road, Cookhill, Alcester,
Warwickshire, B49 5LJ

Introduced and edited by Amelia Carruthers.
Cover design by Zoë Horn Haywood.
Design by Zoë Horn Haywood and Sam Bigland.

British Library Cataloguing-in-Publication Data. A
catalogue record for this book is available from the
British Library.

Contents

An Introduction to
the Fairy Tale

Fairy Tales are told in almost every society, all over the globe. They have the ability to inspire generations of young and old alike, yet fail to fit neatly into any one mode of storytelling. Today, most people know these narratives through literary works or even film versions, but this is a far cry from the genre's early development. Most of the stories began, and are still propagated through oral traditions, which are still very much alive in certain cultures. Especially in rural, poorer regions, the telling of tales – from village to village, or from elder to younger, preserves culture and custom, whilst still enabling the teller to vary, embellish or adapt the tale as they see fit.

To provide a brief attempt at definition, a fairy tale is a type of short story that typically features 'fantasy' characters, such as dwarves, elves, fairies, giants, gnomes, goblins, mermaids, trolls or witches, and usually magic or enchantments to boot! Fairy tales may be distinguished from other folk narratives such as legends (which generally involve belief in the veracity of the events described) and explicitly moral tales, including fables or those of a religious nature. In cultures where demons and witches are perceived as real, fairy tales may merge into legends, where the narrative is perceived both by teller and hearers as being grounded in historical truth. However unlike legends and epics, they usually do not contain more than superficial references to religion and actual places, people, and events; they take place 'once upon a time' rather than in reality.

The history of the fairy tale is particularly difficult to trace, as most often, it is only the literary forms that are available to the scholar. Still, written evidence indicates that fairy tales have existed for thousands of years, although not perhaps recognized as a genre. Many of today's fairy narratives have evolved from centuries-old stories that have appeared, with variations, in multiple cultures around the world. Two theories of origins have attempted to explain the common elements in fairy tales across continents. One is that a single point of origin generated any given tale, which then spread over the centuries. The other is that such fairy tales stem from common human experience and therefore can appear separately in many different origins. Debates still rage over which interpretation is correct, but as ever, it is likely that a combination of both aspects are involved in the advancements of these folkloric chronicles.

Some folklorists prefer to use the German term *Märchen* or 'wonder tale' to refer to the genre over *fairy tale,* a practice given weight by the definition of Thompson in his 1977 edition of *The Folktale.* He described it as 'a tale of some length involving a succession of motifs or episodes. It moves in an unreal world without definite locality or definite creatures and is filled with the marvellous. In this never-never land, humble heroes kill adversaries, succeed to kingdoms and marry princesses.' The genre was first marked out by writers of the Renaissance, such as Giovanni Francesco Straparola and Giambattista Basile, and stabilized through the works of later collectors such as Charles Perrault and the Brothers Grimm. The oral tradition of the fairy tale came long before the written page however.

Tales were told or enacted dramatically, rather than written down, and handed from generation to generation. Because of this, many fairy tales appear in written literature throughout different cultures, as in *The Golden Ass,* which includes *Cupid and Psyche* (Roman, 100–200 CE), or the *Panchatantra* (India, 3rd century CE). However it is still unknown to what extent these reflect the actual folk tales even of their own time. The 'fairy tale' as a genre became popular among the French nobility of the seventeenth century, and among the tales told were the *Contes* of Charles Perrault (1697), who fixed the forms of 'Sleeping Beauty' and 'Cinderella.' Perrault largely laid the foundations for this new literary variety, with some of the best of his works including 'Puss in Boots', 'Little Red Riding Hood' and 'Bluebeard'.

The first collectors to attempt to preserve not only the plot and characters of the tale, but also the style in which they were told were the Brothers Grimm, who assembled German fairy tales. The Brothers Grimm rejected several tales for their anthology, though told by Germans, because the tales derived from Perrault and they concluded that the stories were thereby *French* and not *German* tales. An oral version of 'Bluebeard' was thus rejected, and the tale of 'Little Briar Rose', clearly related to Perrault's 'The Sleeping Beauty' was included only because Jacob Grimm convinced his brother that the figure of *Brynhildr*, from much earlier Norse mythology, proved that the sleeping princess was authentically German. The Grimm Brothers remain some of the best-known story-tellers of folk tales though, popularising 'Hansel and Gretel', 'Rapunzel', 'Rumplestiltskin' and 'Snow White.'

The work of the Brothers Grimm influenced other collectors, both inspiring them to collect tales and leading them to similarly believe, in a spirit of romantic nationalism, that the fairy tales of a country were particularly representative of it (unfortunately generally ignoring any cross-cultural references). Among those influenced were the Norwegian Peter Christen Asbjørnsen (*Norske Folkeeventyr*, 1842-3), the Russian Alexander Afanasyev (*Narodnye Russkie Skazki*, 1855-63) and the Englishman, Joseph Jacobs *(English Fairy Tales,* 1890). Simultaneously to such developments, writers such as Hans Christian Andersen and George MacDonald continued the tradition of penning original literary fairy tales. Andersen's work sometimes drew on old folktales, but more often deployed fairytale motifs and plots in new stories; for instance in 'The Little Mermaid', 'The Ugly Duckling' and 'The Emperor's New Clothes.'

Fairy tales are still written in the present day, attesting to their enormous popularity and cultural longevity. Aside from their long and diverse literary history, these stories have also been stunningly illustrated by some of the world's best artists — as the reader will be able to see in the following pages. The Golden Age of Illustration (a period customarily defined as lasting from the latter quarter of the nineteenth century until just after the First World War) produced some of the finest examples of this craft, and the masters of the trade are all collected in this volume, alongside the original, inspiring tales. These images form their own story, evolving in conjunction with the literary development of the tales. Consequently, the illustrations are presented in their own narrative sequence, for the reader to appreciate *in and of themselves*. An introduction to the 'Golden Age' can also be found at the end of this book.

THE HISTORY OF RUMPELSTILTSKIN

Rumpelstiltskin is a tale of primarily European heritage, dating back to at least the sixteenth century. The story has been studied by many folklorists, the most notable of which has been Edward Clodd, who produced an entire book on *Tom-Tit-Tot* (the English name of the story) titled *An Essay on Savage Philosophy in Folk-Tale* (1898). The legend is indeed 'savage' in parts, encompassing vice-ridden characters, deceit, maleficent goblins and grizzly endings. It takes the form of Aarne-Thompson type 500: 'the name of the helper', as in almost every variant on the narrative, the plot centres around the discovery of the name of a troublesome, though not necessarily evil 'helper'. This assistant is, of course, the Rumpelstiltskin character.

The same story pattern appears in numerous other cultures: *Whuppity Stoorie* in Scotland (from Robert Chambers' *Popular Rhymes of Scotland*), *Gilitrutt* in Iceland, *Joaidane* in Arabic ('he who talks too much'), *Khlamushka* ('junker') in Russia, and *Ruidoquedito* (meaning 'little noise') in South America. The most famous version of the *Rumpelstiltskin* narrative was penned by the Brothers Grimm however, and it was from this tale that most subsequent folklorists took their inspiration. The story was collected in their 1812 edition of the Grimms' *Kinder und Hausmärchen* (Children's and Household Tales), and subsequently revised and refashioned in their final 1857 volume. The narrative was so well known across Europe by this point, that the Grimms actually collected four versions of the legend – which they combined into the Rumpelstiltskin plot best-recognised today.

To give a brief overview of the story, the Grimm's adaptation starts with a miller, who lies to the King that his daughter can spin straw into gold (recalling the mystical and much-sought after practice of alchemy). The King demands that the girl perform this act and shuts her in a tower filled with straw and a spinning wheel, threatening to kill her if she is not capable. Naturally, she has given up all hope until a imp-like creature appears in the room and spins the straw into gold for her, in return for a necklace. This arrangement continues, in successively larger rooms, until the girl has run out of jewellery. The king this time has promised to marry the girl if she completes the task, and so the imp extracts a promise that her firstborn child will be given to him. Time passes, and when her first child is born, the imp returns. The (now-Queen) offers him all her wealth if she may keep the baby. The imp has no interest in her wealth, but offers to give up his claim if the Queen can guess his name within three days...

The name 'Rumpelstiltskin' is thought to have derived from an old children's game named *Rumpele stilt oder der Poppart,* which was mentioned in Johann Fischart's *Geschichtklitterung,* or *Gargantua* (1577). Fischart (1545 - 1591) was a German satirist and publicist, and his game was the 363rd 'amusement' in his book. Still played in some parts of Germany, 'rumpeln' meant *to make a noise,* and 'Stilzer' referred to someone with a limp. The archaic German word 'Stülz' also means 'lame' or 'with a limp', and so 'Rumpelstilzchen' was conceived as a noisy goblin with a limp (directly translating as 'little rattle stilt'). Children would take it in turns to assume the role of the marauding goblin (also called a *pophart* or *poppart*) that makes noises by rattling pots and rapping on planks. The meaning is also similar to *rumpelgeist* ('rattle ghost') or *poltergeist,* a mischievous spirit that clatters and moves household objects.

Although this is the first mention of 'Rumpelstiltskin', Fischart's book was actually a loose adaption of an earlier tome, that of the Frenchman François Rabelais (1483 - 1553). Both these men were skilled satirists and humourists, who took great delight in manipulating and inventing words or phrases. Rabelais's work *The Life of Gargantua and of Pantagruel* (published between 1534 and 1564) told of the adventures of two giants, featuring much crudity, scatological humour and violence. Elements which greatly amused Fischart! This 'crude' beginning helps to explain the format of the *Rumpelstiltskin* narrative as we know it today – there are no beautiful princesses, rescued by knights on horseback. Instead, the story revolves around a young woman (often depicted a lazy and ungrateful daughter), married to a king through dishonest means, and the self-seeking 'goblin' character that provides the dubious 'aid.' Names are also of great significance in folklore; the only character who generally has a name is Rumpelstiltskin (*Tom Tit Tot* in Joseph Jacob's variant, *Whuppity Stoorie* for Robert Chambers, *Kinkach Martinko* in the Slavic tale, or *Titteli Ture* in the Swedish story, the list goes on...). It is only when the young girl discovers the 'little man's' name, that she gains power over him.

The name 'Rumpelstiltskin' could also suggest a darker theme, with 'little rattle stilt' taking on a phallic interpretation. The impish creature 'makes gold' with the young girl each night, and then demands her first born (which may very well be his to take). Thus the story could be interpreted in the form of a 'women's tale'; a forewarning about what married life could be like for a young, un-educated and easily manipulated female. It is only once the girl knows what to call the visiting imp (thus gaining *masculine* knowledge), that she is able to control her own fate. In the Mongolian derivation, *The Use of Magic Language* (the only story to feature a male lead) the Prince is explicitly sent on a quest 'to gain knowledge', before he meets his untimely end. Such elements also suggest a 'shadow-animus' narrative, a coming-of-age tale, where the young protagonist is 'trapped' until they are able to grow into maturity by rebelling against their elders. The young girl (as the character is most often portrayed) has after all been betrayed three times by those in a position of trust; her parent, her husband, and the Rumpelstiltskin character. Three is a highly significant number as well, representative of the Holy Trinity; there are three fairies in Giambattista Basile's Italian variant; three nights of spinning, and three 'gifts' that the young woman must give to Rumpelstiltskin in the Grimms' tale (the necklace, the ring and the first-born child); three guesses allowed by *Tom Tit Tot* (the English variant) and again, three days of captivity in the Slavic tale of *Kinkach Martinko*.

As well as altering the name of the antagonist, the differing versions from Europe and the wider world present the basic narrative in strikingly imaginative ways. Giambattista Basile, a Neapolitan poet and courtier, published the first full-length printed version of the *Rumpelstiltskin-type* narrative in his *Pentamerone* (1634 - 36). Whilst differing substantially from the Grimms' later tale, Basile did introduce the main features of the narrative; the lie about the young girl's ability to spin flax, her subsequent marriage to a wealthy (though demanding) husband, and the 'aid' of the helper (this time fairies, instead of the imp). Crucially though, Basile's story is the only version *not* to have a name-guessing game. The Swedish version presents the Rumpelstiltskin character (named *Titteli Ture*) as an ugly and deformed man, described later in the tale as a dwarf. This change is significant, and arguably a mis-translation, as in the original German, the Grimms referred to Rumpelstiltskin as a 'männlein' (*little man*) as opposed to the word 'Zwerge', meaning dwarf. In traditional fairy-tale narratives, dwarf's are largely irrelevant beings, with little or no magical powers. In contrast, Männlein's are more associated with goodness, for example in the Grimm's *The Three Männlein of the Woods*, the wise and knowledgeable creatures help the young girl to marry the Prince.

Indeed, although he doesn't seem good, Rumpelstiltskin is incredibly knowledgeable, being able to spin the gold that the young woman requires. Spinning itself has obvious connotations with fate (the three fates), as the activity which is used to control people's destinies. If Rumpelstiltskin is thus as wise and as powerful as the imagery would suggest, why does he then give the young woman a chance to escape her fateful promise, and keep her first-born? Rumpelstiltskin could be portrayed as a devil-like character, trying to tempt the woman into the sin of giving up her child. But by offering the woman a chance at 'redemption', his behaviour hints the double-sided temperament of männlein's, fairies, imps and the like, with both good and bad elements to their character. At the end of the Grimms' tale (though not in any others), Rumpelstiltskin symbolically rips himself in two, thus revealing his dual nature. There are no overt morals to the story, it could be read as warning against making promises that can't be fulfilled, or a warning against bragging, idleness or lies, or even a cautionary tale that transformation (turning straw into gold and the girl into a queen), does not come without a price. But, as in all great tales, the exact interpretation is left up to the reader.

As a testament to this story's ability to inspire and entertain generations of readers, *Rumpelstiltskin* continues to influence popular culture internationally, lending plot elements, allusions and tropes to a wide variety of artistic mediums. The tale has been translated into almost every language across the globe, and very excitingly, is continuing to evolve in the present day. We hope the reader enjoys this collection of some of its best re-tellings.

The Seven Bits of Bacon Rind

(An Italian Tale)

The Seven Bits of Bacon Rind was written by Giambattista Basile (1566-1632), a Neapolitan poet and courtier. It was first published in his collection of Neapolitan fairy tales titled *Lo Cunto de li Cunti Overo lo Ttrattenemiento de Peccerille* (translating as 'The Tale of Tales, or Entertainment for Little Ones'), posthumously published in two volumes in 1634 and 1636. Although neglected for some time, the work received a great deal of attention after the Brothers Grimm praised it highly as the first national collection of fairy tales.

Many of the fairy tales that Basile collected are the oldest known variants in existence, including this, the first full-length printed version of a *Rumpelstiltskin-type* narrative. The story differs substantially from the Grimm's better known version, though it also introduces several key tropes: the lie about the young girl's ability to spin flax, her subsequent marriage to a wealthy (though demanding) husband, the 'aid' of the helper (this time some fairies), and as a result of which, the young woman's subsequent life of luxury. Unlike *Rumpelstiltskin*, Basile's fairies ask for nothing in return for their help, and likewise do not suggest the name-guessing game.

➤

Once upon a time there lived a beggarly old woman, who with distaff in hand, dabbling folk with her spittle on the way, used to step from door to door, begging alms, and since by craft and deceit one lives half the year round, she made some women, who were tender of lungs and easy of faith, believe that she was going to do I know not what to fatten a very thin daughter she had. By thus begging, she gained the gift of seven pieces of pig's lard with the skin, which she took home with a quantity of straw and small bits of wood she had gathered by the way. Giving them to her daughter, she bade her cook them, whilst she went and begged of some gardeners an handful of greens to cook with them, and thus to make a tasty dish of food. The daughter took the pieces of skin, and burning off the bristles, put the skins in the pot, and began to cook them. But not so much did they boil in the pot, as they boiled in her throat, because the smell which came forth therefrom was a mortal defiance to taste its flavour in the field of appetite, and an immediate summons to the bank of gluttony, so much so, that after resisting for some time the temptation, at the last provoked by the natural odour that came forth from the pot, and drawn by her natural greed, and pulled by the throat by the hunger which gnawed at her entrails, she let herself slip, and tried a little of it, and the flavour being good, she said to herself, 'Let him that feareth become a bailiff; I am in it for this time; let us eat, and let it come of clay, or nails, or other, 'tis but a pig's skin. What will it be? Whatever may it be? I have good skin upon my shoulders to pay for these skins;' and thus saying, she put down the first, and feeling her stomach gnaw the more, took up the second; and after wards she ate the third, and thus, one after the other, until she had eaten them all. Now having done this bad service, thinking of the error, and dreaming that the skins would stick in her throat, she bethought herself to blind her mother, and taking an old shoe, cut the sole in seven pieces, and put it in the pot.

In the meanwhile her mother returned with a bunch of greens, and cutting them up in small bits with all the suckers, so as not to lose a crumb, when she saw that the pot boiled, she put all the greens therein, together with a quantity of lard, that a coachman, who had it left from greasing a carriage, gave her in alms. Then she bade her daughter lay a coarse cloth upon an old box of poplar wood, and bringing forth from a pair of saddle-bags two pieces of stale bread,

"Five skeins!" cried the King.
English Fairy Tales, 1918.
Illustrated by Arthur Rackham

He one day told the King of the land that his daughter could spin gold out of straw.
Grimm's Fairy Tales, 1903.
Illustrated by Helen Stratton

and taking from a shelf a wooden basin, she cut up the bread within it, and threw upon it the greens with the old shoe- leather, and began to eat. But at the first mouthful she perceived that her teeth were not for shoe-leather, and that the pig's skins, by a new Ovid's transformation, had become the gizzard of a buffalo. Therefore she turned to her daughter, and said, 'Thou hast done me brown, this time, thou whore accursed, and what filthiness hast thou put in the pottage? Has my belly become an old shoe, that thou shouldst provide me with old leather? Quick, do thou confess this moment, how this was done; or say naught, and I will not leave thee a whole bone in thy body.' Saporita (thus was the girl hight) began to deny, but the old woman's vexation increasing, she blamed the smoke which had entered the pot and came forth from it, which had blinded her and caused her to do this evil deed. And the old woman, seeing her food poisoned, and taking hold of a broomstick, began to work in good earnest, and more than seven times did she take it up and let it down, hitting anywhere as it fell.

And the daughter shrieked with loud shrieks, and at her cries a merchant who was passing by entered, and seeing the dog-like treatment dealt by the old woman to her daughter, he took the stick from her hand, and said to her, 'What hath this poor child done to thee, that thou hast a will to slay her? Hast thou found her running a lance or breaking money-boxes? Art thou not ashamed to treat thus a wretched child?' 'Thou knowest not what she hath done to me,' answered the old woman, 'the shameless chit, she can see that I am a beggar, and she hath no consideration, and she would like to see me ruined by doctors and druggists: because having commanded her now that it is hot weather that she should not work so much, so that she should not fall sick, as I have naught with which to feed her, the presumptuous creature, in my despite, would fill seven spindles, risking by doing this to have some bad disease of the heart, and re main some two months in a bed of sickness.' The merchant, hearing this, thought that the cleverness and industry of this damsel could make his house into a fairy's kingdom; therefore he said to the old woman, 'Leave off thine anger and cast it on one side, for I will deliver thee from this danger in thine house by taking this daughter of thine to wife, and lead her to my home, where I will entertain her as a princess, as by grace of Heaven I bring up mine own fowls, and fatten mine own pigs, and keep pigeons, and I can hardly turn round in my house because of its fulness; may the heavens bless me, and the evil eye have no power over me, for I have my casks full of corn, my press full of flour, my pitchers full of oil, my pots and bladders full of lard, and hams and salt provisions hanging by the roof beam, and the rack full of crocks, and heaps of wood, and mounds of coal, and safes of linen, a bed fit for a bride groom: and above all, from rents and interests, I can live like a mighty lord; and besides, I gain safely in these fairs some ten ducats, and if business always went full sail I should soon be rich.' The old woman, beholding this good fortune raining upon her when least she dreamt of it, taking Saporita by the hand (in the Neapolitan custom and fashion), consigned her to him, saying, 'Here she is, may she be thine for many happy years with health and fine heritage.' The merchant threw his arms round Saporita's neck, and carried her home, and he was very anxious for the day to come when he would fare to the market to buy some flax for his wife to spin.

When Monday came he arose early in the morning, and wending where the country-women came, he bought twenty dozens of flax, and taking it to Saporita, said to her, 'If thou hast a will to spin, be not afraid, as thou wilt not find another so madly enraged as thy mother, who used to break thy bones, if thou filledst the spindle; whilst I, for every ten spindle-full will give thee ten kisses, and for every distaff-full I will give thee mine heart; work thou then with a good will, and I will wend to the fair, where I shall tarry some twenty days, and when I return from the fair, do thou let me find these ten dozen of flax all ready spinned, and I will buy thee a fine pair of sleeves of Russian cloth trimmed with green velvet.' 'Thou mayest go an thou art ready,' said Saporita to herself, 'thou hast filled my spindle, yes, run and light the fire. An thou expectest a shirt out of my hands, thou canst provide thyself from this moment

When you have spun all this hemp into gold thread I will make you my wife.
Fairy Tales of the Slav Peasants and Herdsmen, 1896.
Illustrated by Emily J. Harding

She sat there weeping.
Told Again - Old Tales Told Again, 1927.
Illustrated by A. H. Watson

of blotting-paper; thou hast found her, and 'twas milk of the black goat, to spin twenty dozens of flax in twenty days. May evil happen to the boat that brought thee in this country. Go, for thou hast the time, and thou shalt find the flax spun when the liver groweth hair, and the ape a tail.'

In the meanwhile her husband fared on his journey, and she, who was as greedy and gluttonous as she was lazy, did not wait long before she began to mix flour, and take the oil, and cook fritters, and make cakes, and from morning till night she did naught else, but gnaw and munch like a mouse, and eat like a pig. But now when the term arrived of her husband's return, she began to spin very fine, considering the noise and great fracas that would occur when the merchant came back and found the flax untouched, and the press and pitchers empty; and therefore, taking a long perch, wound round it a dozen of the flax with all the tow and the rest, and hanging upon a big fork an Indian vegetable marrow, and tying the perch at one side of the wall of the terrace, she began to lower this father abbot of spindles down the terrace, keeping by her side a cauldron full of macaroni broth instead of the saucer full of water, and whilst she spinned like a ship's rope, every time she dipped her fingers in water she played a carnival game with the passers-by. Now passed that way three fairies, and they enjoyed so much the sight of this ugly vision, that they laughed till they fell back wards: and for this cause they cried, 'May all the flax in that house be found spun, and made into cloth, and whitened,' which thing was done at once, and Saporita swam in the fat of en joyance, sighting this good venture raining upon her from heaven. But so that no more of this kind of enjoyance should befall her from her husband, she let him find her in bed, having first spread on it a measure of hazel-nuts; and when the merchant arrived, she began to lament, and turning first one side then the other she cracked the nuts, which made a sound as if the bones unhinged one from the other; and her husband asking of her how it was with her, she answered him with a very melancholic voice, 'I cannot be much worse, than I am now, O my husband, I have not a whole bone in my body; and what does it seem to thee but a little grass for the sheep, to skin twenty dozen of flax in twenty days, and to weave the cloth also? Wend thy ways, O my husband, for thou hast not paid my mother, and discretion has been eaten by the ass; when I shall be dead, my mother will not give birth to another like me, and therefore thou wilt not catch me any more at these dog's works; and I do not wish to fill so many spindles that I break the spindle of my life.'

The husband made her a thousand caresses, and said to her, 'Be thou well once more, O my darling wife, as I desire much more this beauteous loving frame than all the cloths in the world; and now I know that thy mother was right in chastising thee for so much work, because thou losest thine health. But be of good cheer. I shall spend an eye of my head to get thee back to health, and wait a while, I shall go at once for the doctor;' and thus saying, he went at once to call Messer Cattupolo. Whereupon Saporita ate up all the nuts, and threw the shells out of the window, and when the doctor came, feeling her pulse, and observing her face, and looking in the chamber-pot, and smelling in the night-vase, he concluded with Galenus and Hippocrates that her malady was superfluous blood, and from doing naught; and the merchant, thinking he heard nonsense, putting a carlino in his hand, sent him off warm and stinking; and wanting to go for another physician, Saporita told him that there was no need, because the sight of him only had cured her; and so her husband embraced her, and said that from that time forth she should enjoy herself without work, because it was impossible to have a Greek and cabbages,

'The cask full, and the slave-girl drunk.'

Nothing else was in the room but a spindle.
Old, Old Fairy Tales, 1935.
Illustrated by Anne Anderson

21

Rumpelstiltskin

(A German Tale)

Rumpelstiltskin is a tale collected by the Brothers Grimm, (or *Die Brüder Grimm*), Jacob (1785–1863) and Wilhelm Grimm (1786–1859). It was first published in *Kinder und Hausmärchen* ('Children's and Household Tales') in 1812. *Kinder und Hausmärchen* was a pioneering collection of German folklore, and the Grimms built their anthology on the conviction that a national identity could be found in popular culture and with the common folk (*Volk*). Their first volumes were highly criticised however, because although they were called 'Children's Tales', they were not regarded as suitable for children, for both their scholarly information and gruesome subject matter.

Unlike the Italian version of the tale, the woman in the Grimm's narrative is not portrayed as lazy and greedy, but as a beautiful young woman. Her ability to spin straw is likewise exaggerated – but this time, she is said to be able to 'spin straw into Gold.' In the Grimm's, slightly darker (though less bawdy narrative), she is asked to give something in return for the help received, and trades all her worldly possessions until she has nothing left. In a similar manner to Basile's tale, as a result of this artifice, the girl is subsequently married to the King. She manages to escape the promise she has made to the 'helper', and whilst the tale ends rather well for the young woman, the 'helper' is less fortunate.

>———→

All of a sudden the door opened, and a droll-looking little man hobbled in.
Grimm's Fairy Tales, 1911.
Illustrated by Charles Folkard

Once upon a time there was a miller who was poor, but who had a beautiful daughter. Now it happened that he got into a conversation with the king, and to make an impression on him he said, "I have a daughter who can spin straw into gold."

The king said to the miller, "That is an art that I really like. If your daughter is as skilful as you say, then bring her to my castle tomorrow, and I will put her to the test."

When the girl was brought to him he led her into a room that was entirely filled with straw. Giving her a spinning wheel and a reel, he said, "Get to work now. Spin all night, and if by morning you have not spun this straw into gold, then you will have to die." Then he himself locked the room, and she was there all alone.

The poor miller's daughter sat there, and for her life she did not know what to do. She had no idea how to spin straw into gold. She became more and more afraid, and finally began to cry.

Then suddenly the door opened. A little man stepped inside and said, "Good evening, Mistress Miller, why are you crying so?"

"Oh," answered the girl, "I am supposed to spin straw into gold, and I do not know how to do it."

The little man said, "What will you give me if I spin it for you?"

"My necklace," said the girl.

The little man took the necklace, sat down before the spinning wheel, and whir, whir, whir, three times pulled, and the spool was full. Then he put

The Dwarf appears.
The Old Fairy Tales, *c.* 1900.
Illustrated by John Moyr Smith

another one on, and whir, whir, whir, three times pulled, and the second one was full as well. So it went until morning, and then all the straw was spun, and all the spools were filled with gold.

At sunrise the king came, and when he saw the gold he was surprised and happy, but his heart became even more greedy for gold. He had the miller's daughter taken to another room filled with straw. It was even larger, and he ordered her to spin it in one night, if she valued her life.

The girl did not know what to do, and she cried. Once again the door opened, and the little man appeared. He said, "What will you give me if I spin the straw into gold for you?"

"The ring from my finger," answered the girl.

The little man took the ring, and began once again to whir with the spinning wheel. By morning he had spun all the straw into glistening gold. The king was happy beyond measure when he saw it, but he still did not have his fill of gold. He had the miller's daughter taken to a still larger room filled with straw, and said, "Tonight you must spin this too. If you succeed you shall become my wife." He thought, "Even if she is only a miller's daughter, I will not find a richer wife in all the world."

When the girl was alone the little man returned for a third time. He said, "What will you give me if I spin the straw this time?"

"I have nothing more that I could give you," answered the girl.

"Then promise me, after you are queen, your first child."

Suddenly the door opened, and in stepped a tiny little man.
The Blue Fairy Book, 1889.
Illustrated by H. J. Ford

"Who knows what will happen," thought the miller's daughter, and not knowing what else to do, she promised the little man what he demanded. In return the little man once again spun the straw into gold.

When in the morning the king came and found everything just as he desired, he married her, and the beautiful miller's daughter became queen.

A year later she brought a beautiful child to the world. She thought no more about the little man, but suddenly he appeared in her room and said, "Now give me that which you promised."

The queen took fright and offered the little man all the wealth of the kingdom if he would let her keep the child, but the little man said, "No. Something living is dearer to me than all the treasures of the world."

Then the queen began lamenting and crying so much that the little man took pity on her and said, "I will give you three days' time. If by then you know my name, then you shall keep your child."

The queen spent the entire night thinking of all the names she had ever heard. Then she sent a messenger into the country to inquire far and wide what other names there were. When the little man returned the next day she began with Kaspar, Melchior, Balzer, and said in order all the names she knew. After each one the little man said, "That is not my name."

The second day she sent inquiries into the neighborhood as to what names people had. She recited the most unusual and most curious names to the little man: "Is your name perhaps Beastrib? Or Muttoncalf? Or Legstring?"

But he always answered, "That is not my name."

Suddenly the door opened.
Grimm's Fairy Tales, 1930.
Illustrated by Harry G. Theaker

On the third day the messenger returned and said, "I have not been able to find a single new name, but when I was approaching a high mountain in the corner of the woods, there where the fox and the hare say good-night, I saw a little house. A fire was burning in front of the house, and an altogether comical little man was jumping around the fire, hopping on one leg and calling out:

Today I'll bake; tomorrow I'll brew,
Then I'll fetch the queen's new child,
It is good that no one knows,
Rumpelstiltskin is my name.

You can imagine how happy the queen was when she heard that name. Soon afterward the little man came in and asked, "Now, Madame Queen, what is my name?"

She first asked, "Is your name Kunz?"

"No."

"Is your name Heinz?"

"No."

"Is your name perhaps Rumpelstiltskin?"

"The devil told you that! The devil told you that!" shouted the little man, and with anger he stomped his right foot so hard into the ground that he fell in up to his waist. Then with both hands he took hold of his left foot and ripped himself up the middle in two.

The Girl Who Could Spin Gold

from Clay and Long Straw

(A Swedish Tale)

The Girl Who Could Spin Gold from Clay and Long Straw is a story collected by Benjamin Thorpe (1782 - 1870), and published in *Yule-Tide Stories: A Collection of Scandinavian and North German Popular Tales and Traditions* (1853). Thorpe's source for the story was the Swedish folklore collection, *Svenska Folk-Sagor och Äfventyr* (published in 1844). Benjamin Thorpe had lived in England, Paris and Copenhagen before he began writing on Anglo-Saxon grammar, literature, laws, and folklore. His acclaim as a scholar was such that *Yule-Tide Stories* was featured in Henry Bohn's Antiquarian Library.

In this version of the *Rumpelstiltskin* narrative, the young woman (who is good and amiable, though also indolent) is visited not by an imp-like creature, but by an old man. Instead of weaving the straw himself, he gives her a magical pair of gloves, with which she will be able to complete the task. If she cannot guess his name (the old man is also, 'ugly'), she will have to be his bride. When he eventually finds out that his secret has been broached, the 'old dwarf' instead of driving his foot into the ground with anger, flies into the air – taking the whole roof of the house with him.

➤——→

Tom Tit-Tot.

English Fairy Tales, 1895.

Illustrated by John D. Batten

There was once an old woman who had an only daughter. The lass was good and amiable, and also extremely beautiful, but at the same time so indolent that she would hardly turn her hand to any work. This was a cause of great grief to the mother, who tried all sorts of ways to cure her daughter of so lamentable a failing. But there was no help. The old woman then thought no better plan could be devised than to set her daughter to spin on the roof of their cottage, in order that all the world might be witness of her sloth. But her plan brought her no nearer the mark. The girl continued as useless as before.

One day, as the king's son was going to the chase, he rode by the cottage where the old woman dwelt with her daughter. On seeing the fair spinner on the roof, he stopped and inquired why she sat spinning in such an unusual place.

The old woman answered, "Aye, she sits there to let all the world see how clever she is. She is so clever that she can spin gold out of clay and long straw."

At these words the prince was struck with wonder, for it never occurred to him that the old woman was ironically alluding to her daughter's sloth. He therefore said, "If what you say is true, that the young maiden can spin gold from clay and long straw, she shall no longer sit there, but shall accompany me to my palace and be my consort."

The daughter thereupon descended from the roof and accompanied the prince to the royal residence, where, seated in her maiden-bower, she received a pail full of clay and a bundle of straw, by way of trial, whether she were so skilful as her mother had said.

The poor girl now found herself in a very uncomfortable state, knowing but too well that she could not spin flax, much less gold. So, sitting in her chamber, with her head resting on her hand, she wept bitterly. While she was thus sitting, the door was opened, and in walked a very little old man, who was both ugly and deformed. The old man greeted her in a friendly tone, and asked why she sat so lonely and afflicted.

"I may well be sorrowful," answered the girl. "The king's son has commanded me to spin gold from clay and long straw, and if it be not done before tomorrow's dawn, my life is at stake."

The old man then said, "Fair maiden, weep not, I will help you. Here is a pair of gloves. When you have then on you will be able to spin gold. Tomorrow night I will return, when, if you have not found out my name, you shall accompany me home and be my wife."

In her despair she agreed to the old man's condition, who then went his way. The maiden now sat and span, and by dawn she had already spun up all the clay and straw, which had become the finest gold it was possible to see.

Great was the joy throughout the whole palace, that the king's son had got a bride who was so skilful and, at the same time, so fair. But the young maiden did nothing but weep, and the more the time advanced the more she wept, for she thought of the frightful dwarf who was to come and fetch her. When evening drew nigh, the king's son returned from the chase, and went to converse with his bride. Observing that she appeared sorrowful, he strove to divert her in all sorts of ways, and said he would tell her of a curious adventure, provided only she would be cheerful. The girl entreated him to let her hear it.

Then said the prince, "While rambling about in the forest today I witness an odd sort of thing. I saw a very, very little old man dancing round a juniper bush and singing a singular song."

What will you give me if I spin for you?
Grimm's Fairy Tales, 1922.
Illustrated by R. Emmett Owen

"What will you give me to do it for you?" Said the Hobgoblin.

Grimm's Fairy Tales - Stories and Tales of Elves, Goblins and Fairies, 1917.

Illustrated by Louis Rhead

"What did he sing?" asked the maiden inquisitively, for she felt sure that the prince had met with the dwarf.

"He sang these words," answered the prince,

> Today I the malt shall grind,
> Tomorrow my wedding shall be.
> And the maiden sits in her bower and weeps;
> She knows not what I am called.
> I am called Titteli Ture.
> I am called Titteli Ture.

Was not the maiden now glad? She begged the prince to tell her over and over again what the dwarf had sung. He then repeated the wonderful song, until she had imprinted the old man's name firmly in her memory. She then conversed lovingly with her betrothed, and the prince could not sufficiently praise his young bride's beauty and understanding. But he wondered why she was so overjoyed, being like everyone else, ignorant of the cause of her past sorrow.

When it was night, and the maiden was sitting alone in her chamber, the door was opened, and the hideous dwarf again entered. On beholding him the girl sprang up, and said, "Titteli Ture! Titteli Ture! Here are your gloves."

When the dwarf heard his name pronounced, he was furiously angry, and hastened away through the air, taking with him the whole roof of the house.

The fair maiden now laughed to herself and was joyful beyond measure. She then lay down to sleep, and slept till the sun shone. The following day her marriage with the young prince was solemnized, and nothing more was ever heard of Titteli Ture.

WHUPPITY STOORIE

(A Scottish Tale)

Whuppity Stoorie is a Scottish fairy tale collected by Robert Chambers (1802 - 1871) in his *Popular Rhymes of Scotland* (published in 1858). Chambers was a Scottish publisher, geologist, evolutionary thinker, novelist and editor, who is best known as the author of *Vestiges of the Natural History of Creation*. The book was so controversial (combining theories of stellar evolution and transmutation of species), that Chamber's authorship was not acknowledged until after his death. Thankfully, *Popular Rhymes* was less controversial!

The story is traditionally classed as a *Rumpelstiltskin* narrative, although guessing the name of a helper to rescue a baby is the only main commonality. Akin to Basile's version, the 'helper' is not an imp-like creature, but a fairy. In a similar manner to the Grimm's tale though, the fairy demands the first-born child in return for her help – which can only be prevented by guessing her name. In this tale, it is the fairy that is doing the spinning (not the young woman), as she eventually gives away her hitherto well-kept secret.

➤——→

I see that you are fond of talks about fairies, children; and a story about a fairy and the goodwife of Kittlerumpit has just come into my mind; but I can't very well tell you now whereabouts Kittlerumpit lies. I think it is somewhere in the Debatable Ground. Anyway, I shall not pretend to know more than I

do, like everybody nowadays. I wish they would remember the ballad we used
to sing long ago:

> Mony ane sings the gerss, the gerss,
> And mony ane sings the corn;
> And mony ane clatters o' bold Robin Hood,
> Ne'er kent where he was born.

But howsoever about Kittlerumpit. The goodman was a rambling sort of
body; and he went to a fair one day, and not only never came home again,
but nevermore was heard of. Some said he 'listed, and others that the tiresome
press-gang snatched him up, though he was furnished with a wife and a child to
boot. Alas! that wretched press-gang! They went about the country like roaring
lions, seeking whom they might devour. Well do I remember how my eldest
brother Sandy was all but smothered in the meal-chest, hiding from those
rascals. After they were gone, we pulled him out from among the meal, puffing
and crying, and as white as any corpse. My mother had to pick the meal out of
his mouth with the shank of a horn spoon.

Ah well, when the goodman of Kittlerumpit was gone, the goodwife was
left with small means. Little resources had she, and a baby boy at her breast. All
said they were sorry for her; but nobody helped her -- which is a common case,
sirs. Howsoever, the goodwife had a sow, and that was her only consolation; for
the sow was soon to farrow, and she hoped for a good litter.

But we all know hope is fallacious. One day the woman goes to the sty to
fill the sow's trough; and what does she find but the sow lying on her back,
grunting and groaning, and ready to give up the ghost.

Every morning I'll come to your window and take the flax and bring it spun at night.
The Oak Tree Fairy Book, 1905.
Illustrated by Willard Bonte

I trow this was a new pang to the goodwife's heart; so she sat down on the knockingstone,with her bairn on her knee, and cried sorer than ever she did for the loss of her own goodman.

Now I premise that the cottage of Kittlerumpit was built on a brae, with a large fir wood behind it, of which you may hear more ere we go far on. So the goodwife, when she was wiping her eyes, chances to look down the brae; and what does she see but an old woman almost like a lady, coming slowly up the road. She was dressed in green, all but a short white apron and a black velvet hood, and a steeple-crowned beaver hat on her head. She had a long walking staff, as long as herself, in her hand -- the sort of staff that old men and old women helped themselves with long ago. I see no such staffs now, sirs.

Ah well, when the goodwife saw the green gentlewoman near her, she rose and made a curtsy; and "Madam," quoth she, weeping, "I am one of the most misfortunate women alive."

"I don't wish to hear pipers' news and fiddlers' tales, goodwife," quoth the green woman. "I know you have lost your goodman -- we had worse losses at the Sheriff Muir; and I know that your sow is unco sick. Now what will you give me if I cure her?"

"Anything your ladyship's madam likes," quoth the witless goodwife, never guessing whom she had to deal with.

"Let us wet thumbs on that bargain," quoth the green woman; so thumbs were wetted, I warrant you; and into the sty madam marches.

She looks at the sow with a long stare, and then began to mutter to herself what the goodwife couldn't well understand; but she said it sounded like:

"My necklace," replied the maiden.

Grimm's Fairy Tales, 1903.

Illustrated by Helen Stratton

The little man and the miller's daughter.
The Big Book of Fairy Tales, 1911.
Illustrated by Charles Robinson

Pitter patter,
Holy water.

Then she took out of her pocket a wee bottle, with something like oil in it; and she rubs the sow with it above the snout, behind the ears, and on the tip of the tail. "Get up, beast," quoth the green woman. No sooner said than done. Up jumps the sow with a grunt, and away to her trough for her breakfast.

The goodwife of Kittlerumpit was a joyful goodwife now, and would have kissed the very hem of the green woman's gown-tail, but she wouldn't let her.

"I am not so fond of ceremonies," quoth she; "but now that I have righted your sick beast, let us end our settled bargain. You will not find me an unreasonable, greedy body. I like ever to do a good turn for a small reward. All I ask, and will have, is that baby boy in your bosom."

The goodwife of Kittlerumpit, who now knew her customer, gave a shrill cry like a stuck swine. The green woman was a fairy, no doubt; so she prays, and cries, and begs, and scolds; but all wouldn't do.

"You may spare your din," quoth the fairy, "screaming as if I was as deaf as a doornail. But this I'll let you know: I cannot, by the law we live under, take your bairn till the third day; and not then, if you can tell me my right name."

So madam goes away round the pigsty end; and the goodwife falls down in a swoon behind the knocking stone.

Ah well, the goodwife of Kittlerumpit could not sleep any that night for crying, and all the next day the same, cuddling her bairn till she nearly squeezed its breath out. But the second day she thinks of taking a walk in the wood I told you of. And so with the bairn in her arms, she sets out, and goes far in among

All that night the Queen lay wide awake, a glimmering light beside her bed.
Told Again - Old Tales Told Again, 1927.
Illustrated by A. H. Watson

the trees, where was an old quarry hole, grown over with grass, and a bonny spring well in the middle of it. Before she came very near, she hears the whirring of a flax wheel, and a voice singing a song; so the woman creeps quietly among the bushes, and peeps over the brow of the quarry; and what does she see but the green fairy tearing away at her wheel, and singing like any precentor:

> Little kens our guid dame at hame,
> That Whuppity Stoorie is my name.

"Ha, ha!" thinks the woman, "I've got the mason's word at last. The devil give them joy that told it!"

So she went home far lighter than she came out, as you may well guess -- laughing like a madcap with the thought of cheating the old green fairy.

Ah well, you must know that this goodwife was a jocose woman, and ever merry when her heart was not very sorely overladen. So she thinks to have some sport with the fairy; and at the appointed time she puts the bairn behind the knocking stone, and sits on the stone herself. Then she pulls her cap over her left ear and twists her mouth on the other side, as if she were weeping; and an ugly face she made, you may be sure. She hadn't long to wait, for up the brae climbs the green fairy, neither lame nor lazy; and long ere she got near the knocking stone she screams out, "Goodwife of Kittlerumpit, you know well what I come for. Stand and deliver!"

The woman pretends to cry harder than before, and wrings her hands, and falls on her knees with "Och, sweet madam mistress, spare my only bairn, and take the wretched sow!"

"The devil take the sow, for my part," quoth the fairy. "I come not here for swine's flesh. Don't be contramawcious, huzzy, but give me the child instantly!"

"Ochone, dear lady mine," quoth the crying goodwife; "forgo my poor bairn, and take me myself!"

"The devil is in the daft jade," quoth the fairy, looking like the far end of a fiddle. "I'll bet she is clean demented. Who in all the earthly world, with half an eye in his head, would ever meddle with the likes of thee?"

I trow this set up the woman of Kittlerumpit's bristle, for though she had two blear eyes and a long red nose besides, she thought herself as bonny as the best of them. So she springs off her knees, sets the top of her cap straight, and with her two hands folded before her, she makes a curtsy down to the ground, and, "In troth, fair madam," quoth she, "I might have had the wit to know that the likes of me is not fit to tie the worst shoestrings of the high and mighty princess, Whuppity Stoorie."

If a flash of gunpowder had come out of the ground it couldn't have made the fairy leap higher than she did. Then down she came again plump on her shoe-heels; and whirling round, she ran down the brae, screeching for rage, like an owl chased by the witches.

The goodwife of Kittlerumpit laughed till she was like to split; then she takes up her bairn, and goes into her house, singing to it all the way:

> A goo and a gitty, my bonny wee tyke,
> Ye'se noo ha'e your four-oories;
> Sin' we've gien Nick a bane to pyke,
> Wi' his wheels and his Whuppity Stoories.

A bargain's a bargain.
Told Again - Old Tales Told Again, 1927.
Illustrated by A. H. Watson

THE USE OF MAGIC LANGUAGE

(A Mongolian Tale)

The Use of Magic Language is a tale written down by Rachel Harriette Busk (1831 - 1907) in *Sagas from the Far East, or Kalmouk and Mongolian Traditionary Tales* (1873). The first thirteen tales in the volume are 'Kalmouk' (an old name for a nomadic people of Eastern Tibet), whilst the remaining ten are all reportedly Mongolian. *The Use of Magic Language* is tale fifteen, part of the section described by Busk as 'traceable to Indian sources... [yet having] received an entire transformation in the course of their adoption by their new country.'

Although most of the details of the Rumpelstiltskin narrative are different (unsurprisingly for such a geographical reach), the basic element of the story has stayed the same. Here, a young prince is sent on a journey in order to gain all sorts of knowledge, taking with him a companion. On their return, the companion, being jealous of the Prince's superior knowledge (in a similar vein to the guessing game), kills him. As the prince dies, he utters the word, 'Abaraschika.' When the murderer reaches the palace, he tells the sorrowing King how the prince fell sick unto death, and that he had time to speak only the above word. Consequently, the King sends out his servants (like the Queen in the Grimm's version) to find the meaning of the word; the meaning, once discovered – spells recompense for the murderer.

$$\Longrightarrow$$

53

Round the fire an indescribably ridiculous little man was leaping, hopping on one leg, and singing.
The Fairy Tales of the Brothers Grimm, 1909.
Illustrated by Arthur Rackham

When therefore the Well-and-wise-walking Khan found that he had once more failed in the end and object of his mission, he once more took the way of the shady grove, and once more in the same fashion as before he took the Siddhî-kür captive in his sack. As he bore him along weary with the journey through the desert country, the Siddhî-kür asked if he would not tell a tale to enliven the way, and when he steadfastly held his tongue, the Siddhî-kür bid him, if he would that he should tell one, but give a token of nodding his head backwards, without opening his lips.

Then he nodded his head backwards, and the Siddhî-kür told this tale, saying,—

Long ages ago there lived in Western India a King who had a very clever son. In order to make the best advantage of his understanding, and to fit him in every way to become an accomplished sovereign, the King sent him into the Diamond-kingdom, that he might be thoroughly instructed in all kinds of knowledge. He was accompanied in his journey by the son of the king's chief minister, who was also to share his studies, but who was as dull as he was intelligent. On their arrival in the Diamond-kingdom, they gave each of them the sum with which they had been provided by their parents to two Lamas to conduct their education, and spent twelve years with them.

At the end of the twelve years the minister's son proposed to the king's son that they should now return home, and as the Lamas allowed that the king's son had made such progress in the five kinds of knowledge that there was nothing more he could learn, he agreed to the proposal, and they set out on their homeward way.

All went well at first; but one day passed, and then another, and yet another, that they came to no source of water, and being parched nigh unto death with thirst, the minister's son would have laid him down to die. As he stood hesitating

Round this fire a very curious little man was dancing on one leg.
Happy Hour Stories - Stories from Grimm's Fairy Tales, 1812.
Illustrated by J Monsell

about going on, a crow passed and made his cry of "*ikerek*." The prince now encouraged his companion, saying, "Come but a little way farther, and we shall find water."

"Nay, you deceive me not like an infant of days," answered the minister's son. "How shall we find water? Have we not laboured over the journey these three days, and found none; neither shall we find it now? Why should we add to this death of thirst the pangs of useless fatigue also?"

But the king's son said again, "Nay, but of a certainty we shall now find it."

And when he asked, "How knowest thou this of a certainty?" he replied, "I heard yon crow cry as he passed, 'Go forward five hundred paces in a southerly direction, and you will come to a source of pure, bright fresh water.'"

The king's son spoke with so much certainty that he had not strength to resist him; and so they went on five hundred paces farther in a southerly direction, and then they indeed came upon a pure, bright spring of water, where they sat down, and drank, and refreshed themselves.

As they sat there, the minister's son was moved with jealousy, for, thought he within himself, in every art this prince has exceeded me, and when we return to our own country, all shall see how superior he is to me in every kind of attainment. Then he said aloud to the king's son,—

"If we keep along this road, which leads over the level plain, where we can be seen ever so far off, may be robbers will see us, and, coming upon us, will slay us. Shall we not rather take the path which leads over the mountain, where the trees will hide us, and pass the night under cover of the wood?" And this he said in order to lead the prince into the forest, that he might slay him there unperceived. But the prince, who had no evil suspicion, willingly agreed to his words, and they took the path of the mountain. When they had well entered the thick wood, the minister's son fell upon the prince from behind, and slew him. The prince in dying said nothing but the one word, "Abaraschika."

As soon as he had well hidden the body, the minister's son continued on his way.

As he came near the city, the King went out to greet him, accompanied by all his ministers, and followed by much people; but when he found that his son was not there, he fell into great anxiety, and eagerly inquired after him. "Thy son," answered the minister's son, "died on the journey."

At these words, the King burst into an agony of grief, crying, "Alas, my son! mine only son! Without thee, what shall all my royal power and state, what shall all my hundred cities, profit me?" Amid these bitter cries he made his way back to the palace. As he dwelt on his grief, the thought came to him, "Shall not my son when dying at least have left some word expressive of his last thoughts and wishes?" Then he sent and inquired this thing of his companion, to which, the minister's son made answer, "Thy son was overtaken with a quick and sudden malady, and as he breathed out his life, he had only time to utter the single word, Abaraschika."

Hearing this the King was fully persuaded the word must have some deep and hidden meaning; but as he was unable to think it out, he summoned all the seers, soothsayers, magicians, and astrologers of his kingdom, and inquired of them what this same word Abaraschika could mean. There was not, however, one of them all that could help him to the meaning. Then said the King, "The last word that my son uttered, even mine only son, this is dear to me. There is no doubt that it is a word in which by all the arts that he had studied and acquired he knew how to express much, though he had not time to utter many

Little does my lady dream Rumpel-Stilts-Kin is my name.
Grimm's Fairy Tales, 1925.
Illustrated by Harry Rountree

Rumpelstiltskin Dancing.
Grimm's Fairy Tales, 1899.
Illustrated by R. André

words. Ye, therefore, who are also learned in cunning arts ought to be able to tell the interpretation of the same, but if not, then of what use are ye? It were better that ye were dead from off the face of the earth. Wherefore, I give you the space of seven days to search in all your writings and to exercise all your arts, and if at the end of seven days ye are none of you able to tell me the interpretation, then shall I deliver you over to death."

With that he commanded that they should be all secured in an exceeding high fortress for the space of seven days, and well watched that they might not escape.

The seven days passed away, and not one of them was at all nearer telling the interpretation of Abaraschika than on the first day. "Of a certainty we shall all be put to death to-morrow," was repeated all through the place, and some cried to the *devas* and some sat still and wept, speaking only of the relations and friends they would leave behind.

Meantime, a student of an inferior sort, who waited on the others and learned between whiles, had contrived to escape, not being under such strict guard as his more important brethren. At night-time he took shelter under a leafy tree. As he lay there a bird and its young ones came to roost on the boughs above him. One of the young ones instead of going to sleep went on complaining through the night, "I'm so hungry! I'm so hungry!" At last the old bird began to console it, saying, "Cry not, my son; for to-morrow there will be plenty of food."

"And why should there be more food to-morrow than to-day?" asked the young bird.

"Because to-morrow," answered the mother, "the Khan has made preparations to put a thousand men to death. That will be a feast indeed!"

Rumpelstiltskin.

Grimm's Fairy Tales - Stories and Tales of Elves, Goblins and Fairies, 1917.

Illustrated by Louis Rhead

"And why should he put so many men to death?" persisted the young bird.

"Because," interposed the father, "though they are all wise men, not one of them can tell him such a simple thing as the meaning of the word Abaraschika."

"What does it mean, then?" inquired the young bird.

"The meaning of the word is this: 'This, my bosom friend, hath enticed me into a thick grove, and there, wounding me with a sharp knife, hath taken away my life, and is even now preparing to cut off my head.'" This the old bird told to his young.

The young student, however, hearing these words waited to hear no more, but set off at his best speed towards the tower where all his companions were confined. About daybreak he reached the gates, and made his way in all haste in to them. In the midst of their weeping and lamenting over the morning which they reckoned that of their day of death, he cried out,—

"Weep no more! I have discovered the meaning of the word."

Just then the Khan's guard came to conduct them to the Khan for examination preparatory to their being given over to execution. Here the young student declared to the Khan the meaning of the word Abaraschika. Having heard which the Khan dismissed them all with rich presents, but privately bid them declare to no man the meaning of the word. Then he sent for the minister's son, and without giving him any hint of his intention, bid him go before him and show him where lay the bones of his son, which when he had seen and built a tomb over them, he ordered the minister and his son both to be put to death.

He saw a tiny house in which burned a fire, and round
the fire a little man hopped on one leg, and sang.

The Fairy Tales of Grimm, 1936.

Illustrated by Anne Anderson

"That Khan's son, so well versed in the five kinds of knowledge, would have been an honour and ornament to his kingdom, had he not been thus untimely cut off," exclaimed the Khan.

And as he let these words escape him, the Siddhî-kür replied, "Forgetting his health, the Well-and-wise-walking Khan hath opened his lips." And with the cry, "To escape out of this world is good!" he sped him through the air, swift out of sight.

Tom Tit Tot

(An English Tale)

Tom Tit Tot is an English fairy tale collected by Joseph Jacobs (1854 - 1916) in his *English Fairy Tales* (published in 1890). Jacobs was inspired by the work of the Brothers Grimm and the romantic nationalism common to folklorists of his age; he wished English children to have access to English fairy tales (despite *Tom Tit Tot* being of German and possibly Italian origin!). Jacobs felt that children were too focused on French and German stories; in his own words, 'What Perrault began, the Grimms completed.'

Jacob's version is actually a sophisticated synthesis of the Grimm's and Giambattista Basile's stories. Like the Italian narrative, the young woman is portrayed as lazy and greedy, taking her mother's orders all too literally. But like the German tale, the name-guessing game is crucial to the story. Instead of the young woman's first born being offered up as the prize, it is the woman herself in Jacobs version. The imp is also a lot scarier, with black outstretched hands, and a whirling tale – and the girl must spin flax for an entire month. In a unique departure however, it is the King that discovers the imp's name, unknowingly passing this information onto his new wife.

➤——→

Once upon a time there was a woman, and she baked five pies. And when they came out of the oven, they were that overbaked the crusts were too hard to eat.

Today I brew, tomorrow I bake. The next day the Queen's child I take.
Old, Old Fairy Tales, 1935.
Illustrated by Anne Anderson

So she says to her daughter: "Darter," says she, "put you them there pies on the shelf, and leave 'em there a little, and they'll come again." -- She meant, you know, the crust would get soft.

But the girl, she says to herself: "Well, if they'll come again, I'll eat 'em now." And she set to work and ate 'em all, first and last.

Well, come supper-time the woman said: "Go you, and get one o' them there pies. I dare say they've come again now."

The girl went and she looked, and there was nothing but the dishes. so back she came, and says she: "Noo, they ain't come again."

"Not one of 'em?" says the mother.

"Not one of 'em," says she.

"Well, come again, or not come again," said the woman, "I'll have one for supper."

"But you can't, if they ain't come," said the girl.

"But I can," says she. "Go you, and bring the best of 'em."

Best or worst," says the girl, "I've ate 'em all, and you can't have one till that's come again."

Well, the woman she was done, and she took her spinning to the door to spin, and as she span she sang:

My darter ha' ate five, five pies today.
My darter ha' ate five, five pies today.

The king was coming down the street, and he heard her sing, but what she sang he couldn't hear, so he stopped and said: "What was that you were singing, my good woman?"

The woman was ashamed to let him hear what her daughter had been doing, so she sang, instead of that:

My darter ha' spun five, five skeins today.
My darter ha' spun five, five skeins today.

"Stars o' mine!" said the king, "I never heard tell of anyone that could do that."

Then he said: "Look you here, I want a wife, and I'll marry your daughter. But look you here," says he, "eleven months out of the year she shall have all she likes to eat, and all the gowns she likes to get, and all the company she likes to keep; but the last month of the year she'll have to spin five skeins every day, and if she don't, I shall kill her."

"All right," says the woman; for she thought what a grand marriage that was. And as for the five skeins, when the time came, there'd be plenty of ways of getting out of it, and likeliest, he'd have forgotten all about it.

Well, so they were married. And for eleven months the girl had all she liked to eat, and all the gowns she liked to get, and all the company she liked to keep.

The funniest little black thing you ever set eyes on.
Fairy Gold - A Book of Old English Fairy Tales, 1906.
Illustrated by Herbert Cole

But when the time was getting over, she began to think about the skeins and to wonder if he had 'em in mind. But not one word did he say about 'em, and she thought he'd wholly forgotten 'em.

However, the last day of the last month he takes her to a room she'd never set eyes on before. There was nothing in it but a spinning wheel and a stool And says he: "Now, my dear, here you'll be shut in tomorrow with some victuals and some flax, and if you haven't spun five skeins by the night, your head'll go off."

And away he went about his business.

Well, she was that frightened, she'd always been such a gatless [careless] girl, that she didn't so much as know how to spin, and what was she to do tomorrow with no one to come nigh her to help her? She sat down on a stool in the kitchen, and law! how she did cry!

However, all of a sudden she heard a sort of a knocking low down on the door. She upped and oped it, and what should she see but a small little black thing with a long tail.

That looked up at her right curious, and that said: "What are you a-crying for?"

"What's that to you?" says she.

"Never you mind," that said, "but tell me what you're a-crying for."

"That won't do me no good if I do," says she.

"You don't know that," that said, and twirled that's tail round.

Are you not sometimes called Rumpelstilzchen?
The Fairy Book, 1923.
Illustrated by Warwick Goble

Your name is Tom-Tit-Tot.
English Fairy Tales, 1895.
Illustrated by John D. Batten

"Well," says she, "that won't do no harm, if that don't do no good," and she upped and told about the pies, and the skeins, and everything.

"This is what I'll do," says the little black thing, "I'll come to your window every morning and take the flax and bring it spun at night."

"What's your pay?" says she.

That looked out the corner of that's eyes, and that said: "I'll give you three guesses every night to guess my name, and if you haven't guessed it before the month's up, you shall be mine."

Well, she thought she'd be sure to guess that's name before the month was up. "All right," says she, "I agree."

"All right," that says, and law! how that twirled that's tail.

Well, the next day, her husband took her into the room, and there was the flax and the day's food.

"Now there's the flax," says he, and if that ain't spun up this night, off goes your head." And then he went out and locked the door.

He'd hardly gone, when there was a knocking against the window.

She upped and she oped it, and there sure enough was the little old thing sitting on the ledge.

"Where's the flax?" says he.

"Here it be," says she. And she gave it to him.

"Perhaps," said she. "Your name is Rumpelstiltskin?"
Grimm's Fairy Tales, 1927.
Illustrated by Rie Cramer

Well, come the evening a knocking came again to the window. She upped and she oped it, and there was the little old thing with five skeins of flax on his arm.

"Here it be," says he, and he have it to her.

"Now, what's my name?" says he.

"What, is that Bill?" says she.

"Noo, that ain't," says he, and he twirled his tail.

"Is that Ned?" says she.

"Noo, that ain't," says he, and he twirled his tail.

"Well, is that Mark?" says she.

"Noo, that ain't," says he, and he twirled his tail harder, and away he flew.

Well, when her husband came in, there were the five skeins ready for him. "I see I shan't have to kill you tonight, my dear," says her; "you'll have your food and your flax in the morning," says he, and away he goes.

Well every day the flax and the food were brought, and every day that there little black impet used to come mornings and evenings. And all the day the girl sate trying to think of names to say to it what it came at night. But she never hit on the right one. And as it got towards the end of the month, the impet began to look so maliceful, and that twirled that's tail faster and faster each time she gave a guess.

At last it came to the last day but one. The impet came at night along with the five skeins, and that said:

"What, ain't you got my name yet?"

"Is that Nicodemus?" says she.

"Noo, 'tain't," that says.

"Is that Sammle?" says she.

"Noo, 'tain't," that says.

"A-well, is that Methusalem?" says she.

"Noo, 'tain't that neither," that says.

Then that looks at her with that's eyes like a coal o' fire, and that says: "Woman, there's only tomorrow night, and then you'll be mine?" And away it flew.

Well, she felt that horrid. However, she heard the king coming along the passage.

In he came, and when he sees the five skeins, he says, says he: "Well, my dear," says he. "I don't see but what you'll have your skeins ready tomorrow night as well, and as I reckon I shan't have to kill you, I'll have supper in here tonight." So they brought supper, and another stool for him, and down the two sate.

Can your name be Rumpelstiltskin?
Grimm's Fairy Tales, 1914.
Illustrated by Harry G. Theaker

Well, he hadn't eaten but a mouthful or so, when he stops and begins to laugh.

"What is it?" says she.

"A-why," says he, "I was out a-hunting today, and I got away to a place in the wood I'd never seen before. And there was an old chalk pit. And I heard a kind of a sort of a humming. So I got off my hobby, and I went right quiet to the pit, and I looked down. Well, what should there be but the funniest little black thing you ever set eyes on. And what was that doing but that had a little spinning wheel, and that was spinning wonderful fast, and twirling that's tail. And as that span that sang:

> 'Nimmy nimmy not
> My name's Tom Tit Tot.'"

Well, when the girl heard this, she felt as if she could have jumped out her skin for joy, but she didn't say a word.

Next day that there little thing looked so maliceful when he came for the flax. And when night came, she heard that knocking against the window panes. She oped the window, and that come right in on the ledge. That was grinning from ear to ear, and Oo! that's tail was twirling round so fast.

"What's my name?" that says, as that gave her the skeins.

"Is that Solomon?" she says, pretending to be afeard.

"Noo, 'tain't," that says, and that come further into the room.

"Well, is that Zebedee?" says she again.

A Witch has told you!
Grimm's Fairy Tales, 1932.
Illustrated by Monro S. Orr

Rumpel-Stilts-Kin dashes his foot into the floor.
Grimm's Fairy Tales, 1903.
Illustrated by Helen Stratton

"Noo, 'tain't," says the impet. And then that laughed and twirled that's tail till you couldn't hardly see it.

"Take time, woman," that says; "next guess, and you're mine." And that stretched out that's black hands at her.

Well, she backed a step or two, and she looked at it, and then she laughed out, and says she, pointing her finger at it:

Nimmy nimmy not
Your name's Tom Tit Tot.

Well, when that heard her, that gave an awful shriek and away that flew into the dark, and she never saw it any more.

Kinkach Martinko

(A Slavic Tale)

Kinkach Martinko was written down by Alesander Borejko Chodźko (1804 - 1891), a Polish poet, Slavist and Iranologist. It appeared in *Fairy Tales of the Slav Peasants and Herdsmen* (translated by Emily J. Harding and posthumously published in 1896). Chodźko was a respected scholar, and held the chair of Slavic languages and literatures at the Collège de France; a Parisian school established in 1530 by King Francis I of France.

This tale (although with an unusually violent opening), progresses in a relatively similar manner to most of 'name of the helper' narratives. Like the Swedish variant, the maleficent character is portrayed as small man, but one who asks the young woman to guess the material his boots are made of – *as well as* telling him his proper name. Abnormally for this story-type, a third main character is introduced; another old man, who because of the young girl's kindness (she gives him her dinner), tells her the name of the 'helper.' This is the only example of a *Rumpelstiltskin* narrative, where a character (the second-old man) can be defined as innocent of evil.

$$\blacksquare\!\longrightarrow$$

Once upon a time there was a poor woman who had an only daughter, named Helen, a very lazy girl. One day when she had refused to do a single thing, her mother took her down to the banks of a stream and began to strike her fingers with a flat stone, just as you do in beating linen to wash it.

The girl cried a good deal. A prince, Lord of the Red Castle, happened at that moment to pass by, and inquired as to the cause of such treatment, for it horrified him that a mother should so ill-use her child.

"Why should I not punish her?" answered the woman. "The idle girl can do nothing but spin hemp into gold thread."

"Really?" cried he. "Does she really know how to spin gold thread out of hemp? If that be so, sell her to me."

"Willingly; how much will you give me for her?"

"Half a measure of gold."

"Take her," said the mother; and she gave him her daughter as soon as the money was paid.

The prince placed the girl behind him on the saddle, put spurs to his horse, and took her home.

On reaching the Red Castle, the prince led Helen into a room filled from floor to ceiling with hemp, and having supplied her with distaff and spinning wheel, said, "When you have spun all this hemp into gold thread I will make you my wife."

Then he went out, locking the door after him.

On finding herself a prisoner, the poor girl wept as if her heart would break. Suddenly she saw a very odd looking little man seated on the window sill. He wore a red cap, and his boots were made of some strange sort of material.

He stamped his right foot so hard into the ground with rage that he could not draw it out again.
Grimm's Fairy Tales, 1922.
Illustrated by R. Emmett Owen

"Why do you weep so?" he asked.

"I cannot help it," she replied, "I am but a miserable slave. I have been ordered to spin all this hemp into gold thread, but it is impossible, I can never do it, and I know not what will become of me."

"I will do it for you in three days, on condition that at the end of that time you guess my right name, and tell me what the boots I am wearing now are made of."

Without for one moment reflecting as to whether she would be able to guess aright she consented. The uncanny little man burst out laughing, and taking her distaff set to work at once.

All day as the distaff moved the hemp grew visibly less, while the skein of gold thread became larger and larger.

The little man spun all the time, and, without stopping an instant, explained to Helen how to make thread of pure gold. As night drew on he tied up the skein, saying to the girl, "Well, do you know my name yet? Can you tell me what my boots are made of?"

Helen replied that she could not, upon which he grinned and disappeared through the window. She then sat and looked at the sky, and thought, and thought, and thought, and lost herself in conjecturing as to what the little man's name might be, and in trying to guess what was the stuff his boots were made of. Were they of leather? or perhaps plaited rushes? or straw? or cast iron? No, they did not look like anything of that sort. And as to his name -- that was a still more difficult problem to solve.

*Dashed his right foot so deep into the floor that he was forced
to lay hold of it with both hands to pull it out.*

The Big Book of Fairy Tales, 1911.

Illustrated by Charles Robinson

He was forced to lay hold of it with both hands to pull it out.

German Popular Stories, 1869.

Illustrated by George Cruikshank

"What shall I call him?" said she to herself -- "John? Or Henry? Who knows? perhaps it is Paul or Joseph."

These thoughts so filled her mind that she forgot to eat her dinner. Her meditations were interrupted by cries and groans from outside, where she saw an old man with white hair sitting under the castle wall.

"Miserable old man that I am," cried he; "I die of hunger and thirst, but no one pities my sufferings." Helen hastened to give him her dinner, and told him to come next day, which he promised to do.

After again thinking for some time what answers she should give the little old man, she fell asleep on the hemp.

The little old man did not fail to make his appearance the first thing next morning, and remained all day spinning the gold thread. The work progressed before their eyes, and it was only when evening came that he repeated his questions. Not receiving a satisfactory answer, he vanished in a fit of mocking laughter. Helen sat down by the window to think; but think as she might, no answer to these puzzling questions occurred to her.

While thus wondering the hungry old man again came by, and she gave him her dinner. She was heart-sick and her eyes were full of tears, for she thought she would never guess the spinner's name, nor of what stuff his boots were made, unless perhaps God would help her.

"Why are you so sad?" asked the old man when he had eaten and drunk; "tell me the cause of you grief, dear lady."

For a long time she would not tell him, thinking it would be useless; but at last, yielding to his entreaties, she gave a full account of the conditions under which the gold thread was made, explaining that unless she could answer the little old man's questions satisfactorily she feared some great misfortune would befall her.

The old man listened attentively, then, nodding his head, he said: "In coming through the forest today I passed close to a large pile of burning wood, round which were placed nine iron pots. A little man in a red cap was running round and jumping over them, singing these words:

> My sweet friend, fair Helen, at the Red Castle near,
> Two days and two nights seeks my name to divine,
> She'll never find out, so the third night 'tis clear
> My sweet friend, fair Helen, can't fail to be mine.
> Hurrah! for my name is Kinkach Martinko,
> Hurrah! for my boots are of doggies' skin O!

"Now that is exactly what you want to know, my dear girl; so do not forget, and you are saved."

And with these words the old man vanished.

Helen was greatly astonished, but she took care to fix in her memory all that the good fellow had told her, and then went to sleep, feeling that she could face tomorrow without fear.

One the third day, very early in the morning, the little old man appeared and set busily to work, for he knew that all the hemp must be spun before sunset, and that then he should be able to claim his rights. When evening came all the hemp was gone, and the room shone with the brightness of the golden thread.

*The little man dashed his right foot so deep into the floor that he
was forced to lay hold of it with both hands to pull it out.*

Hansel and Gretel and Other Stories, 1925.

Illustrated by Kay Nielsen

Rumpelstiltskin.

Fairy Tales from Grimm, 1894.

Illustrated by Gordon Browne

As soon as his work was done, the queer little old man with the red cap drew himself up with a great deal of assurance, and with his hand in his pockets strutted up and down before Helen, ordering her to tell him his right name and to say of what stuff the boots were made; but he felt certain that she would not be able to answer aright.

"Your name is Kinkach Martinko, and your boots are made of dogskin," she replied without the slightest hesitation.

At these words he spun round on the floor like a bobbin, tore out his hair and beat his breast with rage, roaring so that the very walls trembled.

"It is lucky for you that you have guessed. If you had not, I should have torn you to pieces on this very spot:" so saying he rushed out of the window like a whirlwind.

Helen felt deeply grateful towards the old man who had told her the answers, and hoped to be able to thank him in person. But he never appeared again.

The Prince of the Red Castle was very pleased with her for having accomplished her task so punctually and perfectly, and he married her as he had promised.

Helen was truly thankful to have escaped the dangers that had threatened her, and her happiness as a princess was greater than she had dared hope. She had, too, such a good stock of gold thread that she never had occasion to spin any more all her life long.

The Golden Age of Illustration

The 'Golden age of Illustration' refers to a period customarily defined as lasting from the latter quarter of the nineteenth century until just after the First World War. In this period of no more than fifty years the popularity, abundance and most importantly the unprecedented upsurge in quality of illustrated works marked an astounding change in the way that publishers, artists and the general public came to view this hitherto insufficiently esteemed art form.

Until the latter part of the nineteenth century, the work of illustrators was largely proffered anonymously, and in England it was only after Thomas Bewick's pioneering technical advances in wood engraving that it became common to acknowledge the artistic and technical expertise of book and magazine illustrators. Although widely regarded as the patriarch of the *Golden Age*, Walter Crane (1845-1915) started his career as an anonymous illustrator – gradually building his reputation through striking designs, famous for their sharp outlines and flat tints of colour. Like many other great illustrators to follow, Crane operated within many different mediums; a lifelong disciple of William Morris and a member of the Arts and Crafts Movement, he designed all manner of objects including wallpaper, furniture, ceramic ware and even whole interiors. This incredibly important and inclusive phase of British design proved to have a lasting impact on illustration both in the United Kingdom and Europe as well as America.

The artists involved in the Arts and Crafts Movement attempted to counter the ever intruding Industrial Revolution (the first wave of which lasted roughly from 1750-1850) by bringing the values of beautiful and inventive craftsmanship back into the sphere of everyday life. It must be noted that around the turn of the century the boundaries between what would today be termed 'fine art' as opposed to 'crafts' and 'design' were far more fluid and in many cases non-operational, and many illustrators had lucrative painterly careers in addition to their design work. The Romanticism of the *Pre Raphaelite Brotherhood* combined with the intricate curvatures of the *Art Nouveaux* movement provided influential strands running through most illustrators work. The latter especially so for the Scottish illustrator Anne Anderson (1874-1930) as well as the Dutch artist Kay Nielson (1886-1957), who was also inspired by the stunning work of Japanese artists such as Hiroshige.

One of the main accomplishments of nineteenth century illustration lay in its ability to reach far wider numbers than the traditional 'high arts'. In 1892 the American critic William A. Coffin praised the new medium for popularising art; 'more has been done through the medium of illustrated literature… to make the masses of people realise that there is such a thing as art and that it is worth caring about'. Commercially, illustrated publications reached their zenith with the burgeoning 'Gift Book' industry which emerged in the first decade of the twentieth century. The first widely distributed gift book was published in 1905. It comprised of Washington Irving's short story *Rip Van Winkle* with the addition of 51 colour plates by a true master of illustration; Arthur Rackham. Rackham created each plate by first painstakingly drawing his subject in a sinuous pencil line before applying an ink layer – then he used layer upon layer of delicate watercolours to build up the romantic yet calmly ethereal results on which his reputation was constructed. Although Rackham is now one of the most recognisable names in illustration, his delicate palette owed no small debt to Kate Greenaway (1846-1901) – one of the first female illustrators whose pioneering and incredibly subtle use of the watercolour medium resulted in her election to the Royal Institute of Painters in Water Colours, in 1889.

The year before Arthur Rackam's illustrations for *Rip Van Winkle* were published, a young and aspiring French artist by the name of Edmund Dulac

(1882-1953) came to London and was to create a similarly impressive legacy. His timing could not have been more fortuitous. Several factors converged around the turn of the century which allowed illustrators and publishers alike a far greater freedom of creativity than previously imagined. The origination of the 'colour separation' practice meant that colour images, extremely faithful to the original artwork could be produced on a grand scale. Dulac possessed a rigorously painterly background (more so than his contemporaries) and was hence able to utilise the new technology so as to allow the colour itself to refine and define an object as opposed to the traditional pen and ink line. It has been estimated that in 1876 there was only one 'colour separation' firm in London, but by 1900 this number had rocketed to fifty. This improvement in printing quality also meant a reduction in labour, and coupled with the introduction of new presses and low-cost supplies of paper this meant that publishers could for the first time afford to pay high wages for highly talented artists.

Whilst still in the U.K, no survey of the *Golden Age of Illustration* would be complete without a mention of the Heath-Robinson brothers. Charles Robinson was renowned for his beautifully detached style, whether in pen and ink or sumptuous watercolours. William (the youngest) was to later garner immense fame for his carefully constructed yet tortuous machines operated by comical, intensely serious attendants. After World War One, the Robinson brothers numbered among the few artists of the Golden Age who continued to regularly produce illustrated works. But as we move towards the United States, one illustrator - Howard Pyle (1853-1911) stood head and shoulders above his contemporaries as the most distinguished illustrator of the age. From 1880 onwards Pyle illustrated over 100 volumes, yet it was not quantity which ensured his precedence over other American (and European) illustrators, but quality.

Pyle's sumptuous illustrations benefitted from a meticulous composition process livened with rich colour and deep recesses, providing a visual framework in which tales such as *Robin Hood* and *The Four Volumes of the Arthurian Cycle* could come to life. These are publications which remain continuous good sellers up till the present day. His flair and originality combined with a thoroughness of planning and execution were principles which he passed onto his many pupils at the *Drexel Institute of Arts and Sciences*. Two such pupils were Jessie Willcox Smith (1863-1935) who went on to illustrate books such as *The Water Babies* and *At the Back of North Wind* and perhaps most famously Maxfield Parrish (1870-1966) who became famed for luxurious colour (most remarkably demonstrated in his blue paintings) and imaginative designs; practices in no short measure gleaned from his tutor. As an indication of Parrish's popularity, in 1925 it was estimated that one fifth of American households possessed a Parrish reproduction.

As is evident from this brief introduction to the 'Golden Age of Illustration', it was a period of massive technological change and artistic ingenuity. The legacy of this enormously important epoch lives on in the present day – in the continuing popularity and respect afforded to illustrators, graphic and fine artists alike. This *Origins of Fairy Tales from Around the World* series will hopefully provide a fascinating insight into an era of intense historical and creative development, bringing both little known stories, and the art that has accompanied them, back to life.

CINDERELLA
AND OTHER GIRLS WHO
LOST THEIR SLIPPERS

SNOW WHITE
AND OTHER EXAMPLES OF
JEALOUSY UNREWARDED

PUSS IN BOOTS
AND OTHER VERY CLEVER CATS

RAPUNZEL
AND OTHER FAIR MAIDENS
IN VERY TALL TOWERS

BLUEBEARD
AND OTHER MYSTERIOUS MEN WITH
EVEN STRANGER FACIAL HAIR

SLEEPING BEAUTY
AND OTHER TALES OF
SLUMBERING PRINCESSES

LITTLE RED RIDING HOOD
AND OTHER GIRLS WHO
GOT LOST IN THE WOODS

BEAUTY AND THE BEAST
AND OTHER TALES OF LOVE
IN UNEXPECTED PLACES

HANSEL AND GRETEL
AND OTHER SIBLINGS
FORSAKEN IN FORESTS